To Isla.
—M.O.

© 2022 Mirelle Ortega

Book design by Melissa Nelson Greenberg

Library of Congress Cataloging-in-Publication Data available.
ISBN: 978-1-951836-57-3

Printed in China

10 9 8 7 6 5 4 3 2 1

CAMERON KIDS is an imprint of CAMERON + COMPANY

CAMERON + COMPANY
Petaluma, California
www.cameronbooks.com

# Magic

## Once Upon a Faraway Land

### MIRELLE ORTEGA

cameron kids

Let me tell you about the place I'm from,
a faraway land brimming with magia.

Powerful magic that twists and turns and
touches everything around you.

It's a place where rain kisses the earth and wild things flourish.

And people turn wilderness into harvest.

A place where my abuelo turned dirt into a sea of golden pineapples, glimmering under the warm Mexican sun.

And my abuelita taught me to string words
together to make up stories.

Where my mamá and tía wove single threads of wool
into the most beautifully intricate blankets.

*mis pájaros azules adorados el otra día en el centro vimos*

And my papá transformed sketches into
stone buildings, bricks into solid walls.

In my faraway land, I saw tiny seeds grow
into shady trees, where beneath I sat and
played on hot summer days.

I also saw little bugs become plagues,
and pleasant rains turned into tropical storms.

And my favorite trees turned into lonely stumps.

I learned that magic isn't good or bad, it just is.
Sometimes it gives. Sometimes it takes.
Sometimes it blossoms. Sometimes it wilts.

And sometimes it is confusing.

The way magic can change things for better
and for worse.

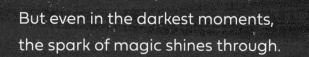

But even in the darkest moments,
the spark of magic shines through.

Like candles in the ofrendas every Day of the Dead.

My abuelo used to say, "There is no harvest without rain."
And there is no sadness that magic can't turn to happiness again.
Even though sometimes it doesn't feel like it.

Sometimes magic is hard to find.

Sometimes magic takes its time.

But it is always there.

Like when people's hands touch the earth and plant seeds that become fruit.

Like when simple ingredients turn
into delicious meals.

Like when strangers turn into friends and houses into homes.

Like when sounds are woven together
into the most beautiful music.

Like when jarochas dance!

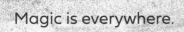

Magic is everywhere.

You can feel it in the air,
even in a new faraway land.

And you can feel it in your fingertips.
Like when blank pages become pictures.

# Author's Note

I wrote my first story when I was twelve. Soon after that, my grandpa said to me, "One day, you should write about us."

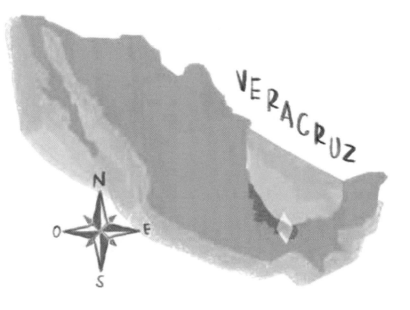

Decades later and many miles away from home, I finally did. I wrote *Magic* to celebrate the place I came from, a small agricultural town called Isla near the Papaloapan riverbank, nestled in the south of Veracruz, Mexico. A paradise of fertile soil and hardworking hands, where I first knew magic. A place that lives inside of me, coursing through my body with every pump of my relentless heart. And though my grandpa is gone, and he can't read this, I feel no sadness about it. I know, with unnatural certainty, that my grandpa didn't need to read this book, because in many ways he wrote it.

My grandpa's hard work wrote this book; my grandma's stories wrote this book; my mom's hugs wrote this book; my aunt's cleverness wrote this book; my dad's imagination wrote this book; my brother's kindness wrote this book, and so on. Their heart is my heart; my hand is their hand. Our words, our story. Us. Magic.

—MIRELLE

the author & her younger brother

Abuelo